THE LOST BONE

AND THE FOUND SISTER

To: Anastasia and Alessandra

Gigi

Mimi

Margo

Numbers 6:24-27

By Margo Smith

WestBow Press books may be ordered through booksellers or by contacting:

WestBow Press
A Division of Thomas Nelson & Zondervan
1663 Liberty Drive
Bloomington, IN 47403
www.westbowpress.com
1 (866) 928-1240

Interior Image Credit: Derek Keijner

ISBN: 978-1-9736-3679-3 (sc)
ISBN: 978-1-9736-3680-9 (e)

Library of Congress Control Number: 2018909725

Print information available on the last page.

WestBow Press rev. date: 9/25/2018

WestBow
PRESS®
A DIVISION OF THOMAS NELSON
& ZONDERVAN

Once upon a time, there were two poodles named Mimi and Gigi.

Mimi was a short gray poodle with big black eyes and fluffy long ears. Gigi was a furry black poodle with very long legs.

Mimi and Gigi were from the same litter, which made them sisters, but they were very different. For instance, Mimi was very prim and proper and acted like a cat. She did not like to get her fur wet or dirty. She only wanted to play outside when the weather was perfect. Mimi's motto was, "No rain, wind, hail, sleet, or snow. Only sunshine at 70°"

In contrast, Gigi was a skillful hunter and loved the outdoors. No matter the weather, she could not wait to be outside chasing chipmunks and rabbits. Gigi's favorite time of year was winter when she rolled in the snow and looked like a decorated Christmas cookie.

Besides loving the outdoors, Gigi also collected dog bones. She had quite a collection. She had ten prized dog bones and lined them up everyday in order to guard them from Mimi.

Gigi's collection of bones was of little interest to Mimi except when she was bored and wanted to tease Gigi. After all, Mimi had her own collection of beautiful hair bows. She wore a different hair bow every day.

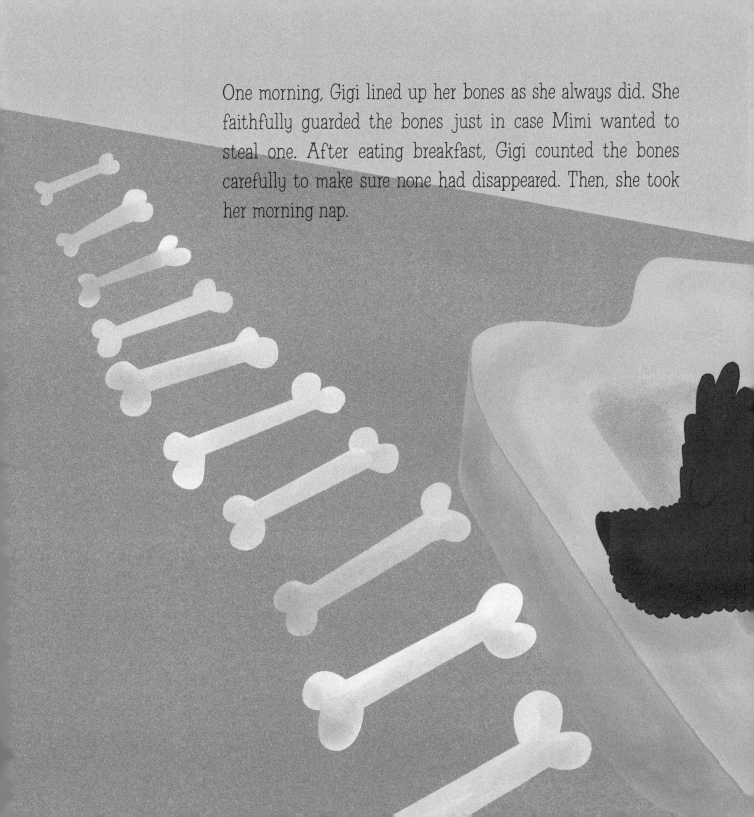

One morning, Gigi lined up her bones as she always did. She faithfully guarded the bones just in case Mimi wanted to steal one. After eating breakfast, Gigi counted the bones carefully to make sure none had disappeared. Then, she took her morning nap.

When Gigi awoke, she decided to go outside. Before going out the door, she looked at her prized bones and counted them again. As she counted, she saw bone number three. This was her most prized bone. Gigi loved this bone the most because it still had the faintest smell of roast beef. It was always so delicious to chew!

Gigi picked up bone number three, and she trotted out the door.

Meanwhile, Mimi was inside watching
the weather to determine if she would
be going outside.

Suddenly, Mimi heard barking and gazed out the window. She saw Mr. C. Chipmunk, their pesky neighbor, stealing Gigi's prized bone while Gigi barked at the redbirds.

Immediately, Mimi ran outside to tell Gigi what happened to her bone. By the time she got outside, Gigi realized her bone was gone and was very upset.

Before Mimi could tell her what happened, Gigi accused Mimi of taking her bone. Mimi was stunned that Gigi thought she had taken her prized bone.

Gigi demanded Mimi return her bone.
As each minute passed, Gigi became
more and more angry with Mimi and
refused to listen to her.

After all, Mimi was jealous of
my bones and always
wanted them

Mimi tried to defend herself, but Gigi became so outraged that she went inside and slammed the door with her paw.

When Mimi came inside, they both went to bed without speaking. In fact, Gigi refused to speak to Mimi for two whole days.

On the third day, Mimi decided to take matters in her own paws. She would visit Mr. C. Chipmunk and get her sister's bone back. When she arrived, Mimi was greeted by Mrs. C. Chipmunk and her litter of pups.

Mr. C. Chipmunk soon arrived and motioned Mimi to follow him to his office. Mimi got straight to the point. She wanted Gigi's bone back. Mr. C. Chipmunk listened patiently to Mimi. When she was finished, he said, "I will give you the bone back for a trade. If you bring me your pretty pink bow, I will give you the bone."

Mimi asked, "You want my pink bow?"

"Yes. I want to give it to my wife for her birthday," replied Mr. C. Chipmunk.

Mimi slowly returned home with great sadness. She knew what she must do; she would take her beautiful pink bow to Mr. C. Chipmunk and trade it for Gigi's bone.

That night, for the last time, Mimi put on her favorite pink bow and looked unhappily in the mirror.

The next morning, Mimi carefully put her pink bow in a bag. Then, she went to see Mr. C. Chipmunk and gave him the bag with her beautiful pink bow.

As he promised, Mr. C. Chipmunk handed Mimi the bone. She took the bone and quickly trotted home to tell Gigi the good news that her bone had been found.

As Mimi put the bone on Gigi's bed, she heard the pitter-patter of her sister's paws. When Mimi turned around, there was Gigi, scowling at her. "I knew you had my bone. Just admit it. You took my bone because you are jealous of me," said Gigi.

Gigi continued, "Now that you have admitted your guilt."

"Wait a minute. I never admitted anything. In fact, you never let me explain," said Mimi.

"There is nothing to explain. You took my bone," said Gigi. "When you admit what you did, we will talk. Until then, I have nothing to say to you." Gigi turned and left the room in a huff.

Gigi would not speak to Mimi no matter how hard Mimi tried. Mimi brought Gigi water and food, and she let Gigi lay on her favorite pillow, but Gigi would not forgive her sister. Mimi did not know what else to do.

As time went on, Gigi grudgingly spoke to Mimi, but it was not the same.

One day, Gigi was outside lying in the sun, and she heard a noise. She raised her sleepy head and saw Mrs. C. Chipmunk scamper across the yard.

Gigi jumped up and ran after the chipmunk. As she turned the corner of the house, there was Mrs. C. Chipmunk picking berries from the holly bush and wearing Mimi's pink bow. At first, Gigi did not know what to think. Then, it dawned on her, Mimi was telling the truth!

As Gigi sat outside, she had a lot to think about. In her heart, she knew Mimi had not taken her bone. It was very different than what Gigi had believed. Gigi was very humbled by her sister's actions.

Before going inside, Gigi made a quick visit to the Doggy Boutique. When Gigi entered the house, Mimi was taking her afternoon nap. Gigi went over to her bed and barked.

As Mimi awoke, she saw Gigi standing over her. *This cannot be good,* thought Mimi. Preparing for the wrath of her sister, Mimi sat up.

Mimi looked at Gigi, and she saw a tear in her eye. Gigi said, "I am so sorry I accused you of taking my bone and did not give you a chance to explain. Can you please forgive me?" Then, she handed Mimi a beautiful package that contained a brand-new pink bow.

The next week, Gigi hosted a party with all their friends and family to celebrate the finding of her bone. At the party, Gigi told all the guests how Mimi recovered her lost bone.

"In particular", said Gigi, "Mimi understood something that I took for granted. She realized friendship and family are more important than possessions. I will always remember what a great lesson I learned from my sister."

"Three cheers for Mimi!" yelled everyone.

As they left the party, Gigi handed each guest one of her prized bones with a note that read, "I lost my bone, but I found my sister."